NO. 1
SPRING 2024

MIDSUMMER DREAM HOUSE LITERARY & ARTS MAGAZINE

CALIFORNIA

Midsummer Dream House
San Diego, California
United States

Cover Photography
by Ashley Kaplan

Paperback ISBN: 979-8-9993991-8-2
Print ISSN: 3064-7819
Printed in the United States

midsummer dream house

CONTENTS

POETRY

MEMOIRS

FICTION

ART

ASHLEY KAPLAN
Bed on the Beach / vi
Photography

BIOGRAPHIES / 64

KAREN PIERCE GONZALEZ

IN MY OPEN HAND

this wandering violin praying mantis is being tuned. Not by me but by the late morning wind that whistles through the minute strings of her spindly, thinner-than-toothpick-body.

Her ornate round head bobs to its beat - one octave higher than any I have ever heard before. The move vibrates her torso, delicately tingling my skin. She tremors ever so slightly. In the sway of her ballet, legs pirouette across my palm. Each spin moves her closer to the cliffs of my fingertips wanting to curl in against the crush of her disappearing. I want to hold her safe from the harms of this world she and I have both been born into.

Unable to camouflage into the fleshy creases of my not-yet-fully-formed fist, she leaps into the air - knobby knees bouncing as she springs away

before I can clutch even one tiny claw.

YOUR BELOVED HEN

plumage petaled in a cardboard box, releases all effort. Her tracks, distinct prints of passage to and from the coop, dissolve with the coming light of the next day; oval eggs will no longer be laid for scrambles, sunny side up souffles.

You squeeze your hands and try to fix what is not broken but done. She is spent. You are spent, too, with sorrow that rolls, like the last penny of a quarter at the feed store, off the counter; disappears into the sawdust floor. In sight of the door to her time here closing, she blinks as you stroke her soft feathers. Her last breath, warm on your wrist.

KAREN PIERCE GONZALEZ

STARLIGHT DRIVE-THRU

The Pleiades in short blue cluster skirts and roller skates, menus in hand, take Friday Night date orders without once peeking to see if anyone's thighs are touching.

And if they had? And if they were?

Kitchen grill chef Taurus sizzles and flips charred comets the star-hop sisters will wrap in fine mesh nets that unfold with the night.

FOUNTAIN PAINT

Those flecks of lint half a mile out in the sleet
are wolves resting with the forest at their backs,
according to the man with the arm-long scope.

We pack drenched snow into hand grenades,
lob them toward the earth's turquoise cauldrons–
Duds, instantly vanished into core water.

At the inn built of last century's trees and
last eon's stone you somehow want ice cream,
licking huckleberry while every crack spreads.

BRAHMS

Preening crows and their porcelain
Maestro's shoes gleam as he tells
Many silver-haired rows glinting opera
Glass lenses at him and me in black
Ciselé over chainmail along the ribs
Balancing a dewdrop of house merlot
About Johannes meeting Ede finding
Csardas composing his first dances
Keeping to pure music in the midst
Of opulence turning yellow in Vienna

We applaud the cellist legs spread
Lovingly under her water gown like
A weaver threads through my armor
Pulling something loose me loose
From the women at my sides with
Older legs and longer testimony
Stitching me tight in to the brocade of
Affirmed harmony under high beams

O.E.L

THERAPY SESSION #1

HOW HAVE YOU BEEN SLEEPING / DESCRIBE YOUR RELATIONSHIP WITH YOUR MOTHER / DO YOU HAVE THOUGHTS OF ENDING YOUR LIFE / DO YOU HAVE A PLAN / WHAT IS IT / DO YOU TALK TO YOUR FATHER / WHY DON'T YOU TALK TO YOUR BROTHER / LIST ALL PAST PSYCHIATRIC MEDICATIONS / DOES YOUR FAMILY HAVE A HISTORY OF MENTAL ILLNESS / OF COMPLETED SUICIDE / HOW DID SHE DO IT / WHAT YEAR WAS IT / DO YOU DRINK ALCOHOL / HOW MUCH / WHY / DO YOU USE DRUGS / HAVE YOU EVER BLACKED OUT / ANY HISTORY OF SELF INJURY / HOW DID YOU DO IT / WHY / LIST ALL POTENTIAL REASONS WHY / DO YOU EVER LOSE TIME / FLASHBACK / FAINT / MAKE YOURSELF THROW UP / HAVE YOU EVER BEEN HOSPITALIZED / ANY PHOBIAS / OBSESSIONS / COMPULSIONS / ANGER ISSUES / WHAT DO **YOU** THINK IS WRONG WITH YOU?

NICK CROMWELL

GHOST HEARTS

I breathe in the crisp air, I breathe out the thought of you. When did I lose time or have I? Was all this you? Or me?

SERAPHINE SAINTCLAIR

THEIR REBORN BLUE

The stars weave their secrets
Into my hair
And I am intoxicated with
Their reborn blue
As I dance the darkness
That I hope has light
Caught in its antlers

DESTINY RITCHIE

GARDENS

Lost in gardens
Carnations
Skin of petals
Sensations

I just want to see them fall
Surround me
The rainbows
Fading

Beds of rhododendron
Thorns of commitments
From apple blossom blushes
To dahlia deceptions

In these gardens
I see you
In these gardens
I want you

Like mazes of maise
And you keep running away
Falling behind
Stuck in place
Rooted to the ground
I listen to the sounds
Distant leaves
Circle around

THOMAS DIMASSIMO

THE UNIVERSE OVER

In the next universe over, you still have my hoodie, because we're still together. Once again, we're sitting in that diner watching Khalil's world crumble after he foolishly orders the disco fries. Our bellies hurt from laughing, but nothing else does. Below the table you stroke my palm with your thumb, and I never let go. We don't know why we're so lucky in the universe over, but it's only because of our failings here. It's okay. We had to learn so they could grow. We exhausted our hearts, so in the universe over, theirs would be made big enough to last.

STRIPED DECK CHAIRS.

The stars weave their secrets
Into my hair
And I am intoxicated with
Their reborn blue
As I dance the darkness
That I hope has light
Caught in its antlers

BERNARD PEARSON

NIGHT TRAIN

So many tunnels
For the red eye
Of grief to go through
Sometimes the dark
Is all consuming
A night of no moon
Where every star
Has crawled away
To the end of the universe
And died and then
There is a glint upon
The window as it
Hurtles who knows where
Its as if those who
have gone before
have made sure the track
is clear

JOHN GREY

COLLECTING EGGS

Now I ask myself,
like a firefly from a dark place,
the dutiful son,
like a reed would bend if it were my spine,
neither monumental nor humdrum,
on my walk from the house to the barn,
swaying in the wind,
everything at such a height,
full of days like the color blue,
nights I listen to as they die in my arms
          come sleep,
I represent no more than
my youthful imaginings –
simply what I am,
my regards.

ANDREW BUCKNER

"SUCH IS LIFE," THE SLITHERING CENTURIES WHISPER

Wheels squeak, a wild animal
in winter snow, a gory streak,
the wagon painted red, a thought

as the mustachioed man,
gray hair twirling merrily
around his quivering lips scans

the exterior, horses snort,
the lonely,
claustrophobic landscape transports

his mind to the stars, his true home,
his time machine avalanches
as the aliens, dinosaurs, humans he

amassed, collected throughout the centuries
he traveled, are footprints bearing down on him,
breathing down his neck, a mark, a fear,

a vision of a future world drowning in content
without a raft, without a sense of artistic
appreciation for craft, confident storytelling

swirls in his brain, his senses, a cold chill
summons zombified goosebumps to rise
on dead flesh as he sees a man, a 21st century one

with his face, struggling for words, struggling
to create long after he has said all that he has to say
so he experiments with the same sentiments, content

(there's that word again)

while struggling to stay afloat in a sinking ship of accruing,
increasing expenses, all cast towards luxuries the world
forces the hands, the eye, the heart of the modern mortal

to worship, to believe is worth an entire lifetime of struggle
and he sees romance, fleeting, children growing, budding
between his arms and loss, inevitable, as is the case in all

the centuries he has traveled, but still he returns to the footprints
and thinks of its symbolism of movement, progress, possible
accompaniment as he looks to see the blizzard encasing his feet,

a gasp forming, another thought that this tale should have some type
of moral, lesson, climax, revelation here, but the wind is howling and
snow keeps falling and time keeps boxing him in.

"Such is life," the slithering centuries whisper.

"Such is life," he pens.

KUSHAL PODDAR

ON A SLOW GLOAMING

To Rijurekh da

The thin light from the window
sniffs, recognises the smoky petrichor
rising from my mellow core.
In the garden I buried my lies, fed by kitchen rot grows
a Pinocchio reed.
If you stare hard; eyes blur; ‘I’ dissolves
freeing you to see more in one, how a reed holds
some infinite reeds, possibilities,
as if a lie can be true when its turn arrives.

NEW CEREMONIES

Ritualistic devourment of the moon, or something like that.
They told me this is how to find a spouse, but I wasn't listening.
I seldom do, there is some kind of block in my brain.
An old brick wall with no rusted gate to swing.
An absolute terror field against ingesting knowledge.
But the moon has been bright in my belly for days,
and the forest outside is dark.

Inside, I sit directly on the soiled hardwood,
it repeatedly creaking beneath my ass with every sloppy shuck of skin
to expose the dirty white bones in my unringed left hand.

There are new shapes in the mounds of discarded flesh and blood.
Visions of a new lover,
some eight foot tall latex skinned absolute string bean of a being
just oozing through the window to palm at my jaw,
to inspect my teeth and tongue, to drool into my open mouth.
Nuptials sealed with a ceremonial viewing of the new lunar light
gleaming through a newly occupied mouth.

ALEX CARRIGAN

ANXIETY SOUNDS LIKE A WHINNY

"When a horse is at full gallop,
there is a moment when all four hooves
are off the ground.
Eadweard Muybridge won a bet by figuring
that fact out, setting up dozens of cameras
and tripwires to go off
when a horse galloped down a road.
This helped kickstart a new art form in the process."

I hope that counts as something
you don't know. When you asked me to
tell you something you don't know,
that fact was the first to come to mind.
I've never ridden a horse, nor have I ever
made a movie that wasn't filmed on a smartphone,
but I'd like to think I enlightened you
further by telling you that.

Maybe it had nothing to do with
our conversation up until this point,
but I hope that it revealed something about me
to you that you never picked up on before.

Maybe I know more about horses or
19th-century photography or early cinema.
Maybe all the afternoons I spent prowling
Wikipedia after school instead of joining clubs
or making friends would at least
extend the length of our conversation here.

You say to me,

"Ok? Wouldn't that be the same for a human as well?"

ANXIETY SOUNDS LIKE A WHINNY

I remain in place,
my hand wrinkling from the condensation
on my glass. You stare at me and
wait for a response. I try to visualize what
it looks like when someone's running.
You could probably set trip wires and cameras
of Usain Bolt running and get the same result.
You continue to look at me while
I construct the film in my head.

Should I tell you about this visual,
or do you want another fact?
Or do you want me to go away
so you can talk to someone more interesting?

I can do both.
Tell me what you want me to do.
Or rather, tell me,
because I don't know what to do.

After Ada Limón

GRANT SHIMMIN

WOULD I HAVE TAKEN YOUR PICTURE ON MY PHONE IF YOU'D BEEN STILLBORN IN THE DIGITAL AGE?

I certainly wouldn't have tweeted it
But I know I could never have deleted it
The guilt and the regret would have been too much
So I'd have held the pain as close as the merest finger touch
What if I'd lost it in transition between phones
And had to learn to find my dead son in the cloud to bring him home?

If I had taken your picture on my phone
I'd have a three-decade-old picture of my pain, unchanged
Unlike me, I'm twice as old, twice more a father, love untold
But would it have brought me healing, there to look at every day
You at peace, red-haired, with eyes never to see?
Or simply kept the pain in place,
Wishing every time I looked for changes I could never make?

If I had taken your picture on my phone, would I have captured your mother's loving look?
As she spoke to you her sadness, as we wished you could respond
But your head bowed down upon your chest would stay
Would it have helped us stay together,
been a tension strung between us?
If she had asked me to take that picture on my phone
There would have been no hesitation bar the framing

Would I have taken your picture on my phone if you'd been stillborn in the digital age?
I can't be sure but I hope not
Though many will, I have no doubt
and who could blame them?
I never thought of inking footprints, taking moulds of your slender, soft-nailed hands
In my heart there lives a picture of your gorgeous baby shoulders, head inclined

towards your feet
Tiny and perfect, in your Mum's words, is how you'll ever be
Would I have taken your picture on my phone? I'm so grateful that I never had the choice

First published in *Does it Have Pockets?*

GRANT SHIMMIN

TOO SOON

Neck stretched across the wide metal bowl, he laps from the far end, head up like his wild cousins, scanning for any danger the kitchen cabinets may harbour. Sometimes a front paw measures the level, especially during those long late-night sessions that suggest his kidneys are on the clock. Now he sleeps, next to the hoodie I discarded on the couch when dawn's chill ebbed, the blanket cascaded down the arm. One eye half-open, front legs tucked in, pointing tail-wards, like an exhausted double dab. I came late into his long life, though before he was over nipping newcomers, or remodelling rodents. I leapt the first hurdle, the rodents rest easier, though hubris remains unwise on either front. Too soon, this will be a poem of memory. I will understand how much I have come to love him, and be undone

BART EDELMAN

OLD TRICKS FOR A NEW DOG

Settled in quite nicely—
Retired from the workforce.
No old tricks for this new dog.
I can bark as long as I like.
The nearest neighbor is deaf,
Living across from the fire station.
It's a perfect marriage, indeed,
Unlike what I had to endure,
Those troublesome years ago.

But that's all behind me now.
I'm leashless, fat, and happy,
Content to travel in any direction
I choose to sniff out;
I'm not the least bit picky.
I eat whatever I find handy
And can't conceive of starvation.

So it's just me and my pals.
When the mood strikes us,
We howl it up plenty good
And won't roll over for anyone—
Least of all, the long arm of the law.
Yet I warn you, in kindness,
Stay a safe distance away.
I may bite the hand feeding me—
Out of pleasure, not spite.

EVAN ELSASS

FISH LIKE FIRE

What I remember most was the pond in my grandparents' backyard, where I'd catch silver jaw minnows. I remember the vague sensation of being young. I remember I was intoxicated by their scales— the way they seemed to chemically react with the light. I'd circle the pond for hours, combing the bank, pulling up their shimmering bodies in a butterfly net. My grandmother kept an empty red Folgers can for me in the garage. "This one," she'd say, "this one I saved so you can keep it for your fishies." After I'd caught enough minnows, I'd sit on the bank, my eyes fixedly gazing down as I watched them swim together in the red-tinted water that filled the Folgers can. I'd hold them under the light of the sun, positioning my head at just the right angle, careful not to cast my shadow over them. The minnows swam together through the light. Their bodies radiated like prisms. I was amazed that fish could look like fire.

My grandmother would watch me from the kitchen window in front of the sink. Over the sound of the hot running water, as she washed the dishes, she'd yell out to me, "Honey, just remember those fish are wild. You can catch them! But you can't keep them!" I poured them back into the pond. As the water trickled down from the can, it churned up the muck of the shallow water by the bank. Obstructed in a cloud of the trembling Earth, the minnows disappeared, raptured below the dark water.

At the hospital beside my Grandmother's bed, these are the things I thought of: minnows, her voice through the kitchen window, and the dark water. After a stroke, my grandmother was unable to speak before she died. When people imagine themselves on their deathbeds, they often think of what their last words will be. But more common the case is, I believe, that before death, the dying are speechless. My family and I each took turns who would spend the night at the hospital. We didn't want there to be a chance of her dying alone. Hospitals are sterile and so unlike the Earth. I had trouble sleeping. Awake beside her in the dark hospital room filled with the hum of machines, I thought of the pond, the minnows, and her voice through the kitchen window.

Honey, just remember those fish are wild.
You can catch them. But you can't
keep them.

At noon, my father came to the hospital so I could go home and rest. When I woke up in the late afternoon that day to a call from my father, he told me my Grandmother had passed. "She looked peaceful," my father had told me. I imagined her last untamable breath. I imagined that it swam wildly from her lips. I remembered the silver minnows pouring into the pond, obstructed in a cloud of the wonderful and trembling Earth.

CHAPEL HILL

In our village Chapel Hill is legendary. It is a gateway of sorts, leading out of our steep sided valley and onto the main road heading north or south. It is how we leave and how we return. For centuries countless feet have trudged up the hill: the miners, farmers, foresters and priests, the midwives, shopkeepers and just about anyone else that ekes out their living in this little corner of the world. Tourists try the hill on the way to the pub from the little campsite and always arrive flushed, thirsty and in a flurry of anoraks and latches.

You and I have walked together up and down Chapel Hill ever since you were born.

It starts at the chapel, now just a shell of a place, with its grand entrance, high windows surrounded by low, moss covered drystone walls. Not that long ago you could round the corner onto Chapel Hill with the pomp of a singing congregation to accompany you on the first push up the steepening slope. Now there's a silence, but for the whistle of the buzzards high overhead or the rattle and clank of a bouncing tractor in the far fields.

I held your little hand the very first time you tried the hill and you twisted and lingered, paused and looked; a wild curious mind taking in the day. You stared up the road, seeing a mountain, with your eyes wide and your button nose dribbling. I slowed my pace and waited as you tottered. We conquered it together.

Once the first curve is behind us the steepness becomes more noticeable. By the terrace where Nick lives, tapping on his drums, or where Tony, a ball of pure energy who eats the hill for breakfast, rents his annexe from Cath and Phil, the edge of the chapel wall ends and the graves crouch back down out of sight. As the hill winds on, the fog of breath grows thicker with effort. With every step there is a feeling of surfacing from the valley bottom; breaking through some invisible ceiling and outrunning the churchyard.

When you started school we stumbled up there for the bus. I worried and fretted that you'd be okay, that you'd make friends and not be cast down by teachers or treated meanly by your fellows. You were stoic, I remember, in your over-sized coat whose arms continued past your hands. Your little bag contained many treats and you wore it on your back like all the kids do. That bag bounced up and down as you hopefully bobbed, but you occasionally dawdled vulnerably and compounded my concern. I was your protector who wanted to carry you in my arms, though all I could do, I knew for certain, was to wait as you dragged yourself up there under your own steam. I didn't walk down until the bus was out of sight.

The little rivulets of water that trickle down the side of the road flow faster as we climb and then, as if to offer some little physical gift, pool slightly as the incline reduces at the modern bungalow with its utilitarian grounds. By now you can hear the rushing of the cars, always going just a bit too fast and acting as an acoustic metaphor for our transition from peace into the modern world. Here, most of the houses have bird feeders and the nervous flitting of the passerines draws our attention away from the cliff-like loom of the road ahead that suddenly rears up again. The dark crows balance on the telephone wires and watch the small birds with what looks like disdain.

Your first fight shocked me of course. I didn't see clearly enough that you were stronger and taller, your strides more assured. To me you weren't ready for this and why should you be? Why should it come to you at all, ever? As we climbed I constantly checked you were okay and that you could cope with another day at school. Did you mind seeing him again? Was he bullying you? "It's okay dad, don't worry, I'll be okay" you replied, but you looked harassed and downcast and were beyond my reach, living in another world; your own world in fact.

Near the top, the round mirror that sits on a post and guides out the reversing cars reflects us back in wide angle. The image bows out and distorts and we rush into view and pass in the blink of an eye. One time as we struggled to the point where legs start to burn, I noticed myself and you alongside. You were formed now, a man; solid and springy. You still had time to grow, but there you were, almost my height, arms swinging, stalking not walking. You were shoulder to shoulder with me, keeping up and smiling. I saw my own father next to you, my head ever so slightly lowered.

I don't suppose you remember the first time I asked you to slow down? I wasn't really interested in those little ferns that grow out of the grey wall with its funny cap of render. No, I needed to catch my breath. We were talking about university and you asked many questions about what it would be like. Actually, I lied when I said it would be nothing but good. I brushed the heartache and worry under the carpet and stuck to the basics. I couldn't imagine your leaving, and, in truth, I was thinking more about me than you. I had never before been the last duck on the beach, watching as the rest of the flock flew away in formation towards exotic lands. I stared at the ferns and panted. You waited with a head full of the future and to you nothing had happened but us walking the hill again.

At the very top the road curls cruelly round with a tiny encore that spills us out on to the pavement of the A44. Before, we would look at each other smirking, amused at this final blow, grabbing above our knees to help our fiery legs cope with those last two steps to deliverance. We'd brush ourselves down and stagger in comfort, on the flat, to our destination. Now, before your body leaves, your mind is living elsewhere. You live away, somewhere faster, more consuming and you've no time to dwell on that little bump on the corner of the road. For you, this place is altering into a memory. Perhaps you will speak about it to your new friends if you find time? Perhaps you might think of the valley before you drift off to sleep? For me you will always be here like Chapel Hill.

Before you left I wanted to drink with you, so we set out for the hill. We passed the huge chapel with its broken windows and rotting plaster. The gravestones sagged and slumped and something was banging in the wind. It was drizzling and it was cold; our breath puffed out like steam trains. And when we reached the bungalow I noticed your shoulder. Your left shoulder was in front of me. I breathed deeply and pushed harder, but there it remained, possibly a foot ahead. You were charging along, light in your step and free. The tie that bound us together on our struggle up the hill was gone. We were no longer walking side by side.

SPECTRA SPRAY

It feels like it was just yesterday, Dr. Sue Bright created “SpectraSpray.” A drug so revolutionary when spritzed into the eyes, it rewired them. Dormant genetic codes were temporarily activated and gave users access to an otherworldly range of colors—ultraviolet blues, infrared reds, and everything in between. This experience, known colloquially as “colour drunk,” also induced euphoria, dizziness, and cognitive impairment.

“Hello. My name is Alex. I’m an avid adventurer in neural landscapes, and I’m a spectraddict. I was among the first to try it. The colors were indescribable, like visual music to my soul. Over time, the euphoria waned, but my tolerance grew and allowed me to remain conscious when others would pass out.

Then, things changed. During a session, faint outlines appeared in my altered vision—wispy figures that danced at the periphery. The more I used, the clearer they became.

Today, the figures manifested again, sharper than ever. One of them stepped forward and beckoned. Its form was translucent and pulsed with a color I’d never seen.

It reached out and touched the air, causing ripples that resonated with my own DNA. A flood of images poured into my mind—astral realms, energy grids, interconnected dimensions. In an instant, I understood: these were not ghosts, but entities from another spectrum of reality, previously invisible to us.

As the figure returned to the others, it gestured one last time—a warning or a salute, I cannot be sure. Then, as quickly as they’d appeared, they vanished. I was alone in my room once more.

So, I tell you this: SpectraSpray has not just expanded our vision; it has torn a hole in the fabric of our reality. These beings, whatever they were, existed alongside us unnoticed—until now.

Do we dare tear up the rulebook and venture further into this uncharted landscape?”

This was Alex’s sixteenth group, and he was met by the usual shock, gasps and intrigue. He thought at least four would sign up. Two were maybes, he could get those with another session or two. Only three were still determined to quit. For now...

As he signed up the eager candidates, the heavy doors swung open with a loud boom.

"FBI! FREEZE!"

What a disappointment. Alex sighed and threw a spectra canister he'd created. It burst and filled the room with SpectraSpray. It was easy to slip away when everyone else is too high to notice. He felt a cold hand on his shoulder. Impossible.

THE KIDNAP

'Mum, help me.'

'Lorna?'

Why was my daughter calling from a private number?

'Mum, help me.'

'Lorna, darling, stay calm,' I said, not-very-calmly. 'Tell me what's happened.'

'What's going on, Mummy?' demanded my younger daughter, Sophie, from across the table. 'What's wrong with Lorna?'

'Lorna?' I asked. 'Are you there?'

She was crying in a way she hadn't done since she was a much younger child. Then I heard another voice. A male, with a transatlantic accent, telling Lorna to lie down and stop struggling.

There was a whooshing in my head and nothing felt real. It was like the time I fell down the stairs and broke my leg: adrenaline temporarily shielding me from the pain.

The man was speaking. 'I have your daughter.'

In my local McDonalds, at two o'clock in the afternoon, I was being told my thirteen-year-old child had been kidnapped.

On the next table, a group of teenagers, all in black like a murder of crows, were talking and playing videos on their phones. Their noise was obliterating what the man was saying.

'Turn the sound down,' I yelled at the teenagers, who turned en masse.

'Take some HRT,' one shouted, and the others laughed.

Sophie was staring at me, the remains of her Happy Meal spread out in front of her, ketchup on her chin.

'Mum, you need to give him money.' Lorna again. 'If you don't, he'll hurt me.'

I told her everything would be fine. I would sort it; that's what mothers did. I asked her to please tell the man to speak to me.

'You need to drive to an address, I'll text it,' he said. 'Bring £500,000. If you tell the police, you won't see your daughter again.'

'I don't have £500,000.'

A pause. '£250,000; final offer.'

'The most I could access would be £60,000 – I can transfer more later.' I had no idea how I could do that, but it wasn't important now. 'I promise, I'll do whatever you want to get Lorna back. Please, please don't hurt her. She's just a child.'

'Bring the money, or you will never see Lorna again. Wait for the text.'

'Help me, help me,' Lorna shouted.

The call ended and the adrenaline stopped shielding me. The pain as intense as the crowning of a baby, I screamed.

'Mummy!' Sophie ran to me and I held her, my face buried into her black hair that was so like Lorna's. A woman in a long puffa coat asked what was wrong, and a young man in a McDonald's uniform who had been sweeping the floor hovered. Others were watching me. The whole top floor of the restaurant seemed to have gone quiet; even the teenagers had turned off their videos.

I stumbled out the story. The puffa-coat woman said she'd call the police, and I told her the man had said not to. She looked unsure.

'Where was your daughter when it happened?' she asked, and I said on a residential trip with the Scouts. She was due back tomorrow. How could they have let this happen?

Help me, help me.

My phone beeped. The text was from a private number too. The address was an industrial estate; Google Maps would have heard of it. First, I had to get money. But what to do with Sophie? I couldn't put her in danger.

The young man in the uniform was talking in an Eastern European accent about AI; I didn't understand what that had to do with me. Other people were asking how they could help. The woman in the puffa coat was comforting Sophie, trying to get her to drink her milkshake. I stood, grabbing our coats from the backs of our chairs.

'We need to go, sweetheart,' I told Sophie. 'Bring your drink.'

Sophie was crying, but I couldn't make her feel better. No time. I had one child who was safe, and one child who wasn't; Lorna had to be my priority.

Help me.

I was strapping Sophie into her car seat, the empty drink cup discarded on the floor, when a voice said: 'It could be an AI scam.'

It was the young man in the McDonald's uniform; he had followed us to my car.

'They happen often at present,' he said. 'There was article in news.'

He said more, but the words flew past me. I ignored him, not caring how rude I was being. My daughter had been kidnapped. I had heard her voice. I couldn't chat about artificial intelligence when she needed me to save her life.

'Mummy, I'm scared,' Sophie wailed as I drove out of the car park.

'It's okay,' I said, clinging onto calm like a blossom to a barbed-wire fence. 'It's okay, darling, Mummy is sorting everything out. Trust Mummy. It's a misunderstanding, that's all.'

'But where are we going?' she asked.

I told her we were going to her dad's. I told her to watch a Netflix show on her tablet so I could concentrate on driving. Soon rawboned American voices were filling the car.

A tight headache pressed between my eyes as we passed the park where I used to take both girls, and now only took Sophie. In the squally weather the last leaves hung on tensely, dead ones thick on the grass. Lorna had done a clear-up of leaves earlier in the year for some Scouts badge.

Scouts.

I had dropped Lorna at the residential centre last night; she was due back tomorrow morning. They hadn't told me she was missing. Had they, somehow, not realised? Or had they been trying to get through to break the news while I was on the phone to the kidnapper? But why wasn't there a voicemail? Why didn't they keep trying?

Was the young man right? Was this a scam? I knew nothing about AI scams, and now wasn't the time to research them. But how could it be fake? I'd heard her voice. I knew my daughter's voice.

My phone rang, and I answered on hands-free.

'If you don't get here soon, I will pump your daughter full of drugs and drive her to Scotland. Her body will be dumped in the North Sea.'

'I'm on my way to the bank. Let me speak to her.'

'Mummy, help me.' She hadn't called me Mummy since primary school, but it was Lorna. I would know my daughter's voice anywhere: any mother would.

'Lorna, I love you. I'm coming.'

'Bring the money: now.' The man again.

'I need to drop my younger daughter at her dad's,' I said to him. 'Sophie can't come to hand over the money. She's only eight.'

'Mummy, help me, help me.' Lorna.

I was hooted at twice as I drove. I broke the speed limit, and would have gone faster had it not been for Sophie. In my head, the words *Help me* played on repeat.

'What are you doing here, Suze? It's not my weekend.'

A Jack Russell barked furiously from Kevin's neighbour's front window, and Sophie shrank into me.

'I need you to take Sophie for a couple of hours. Please, Kevin. I wouldn't ask if it weren't important.'

'I'm about to leave for the match.' Kevin indicated his blue-and-white Brighton & Hove Albion shirt.

'Sophie, sweetheart, go into Daddy's house and watch telly while we chat for a minute,' I said.

'I'm on my way out, Suze.' Kevin spoke through gritted teeth. 'Next weekend is my weekend, as you know; it's in the diary. The diary you set up.'

'I want to come with you to find Lorna, Mummy.' Sophie was crying again.

'Find Lorna?' Kevin frowned. 'I thought she was at a Scout thing.'

'Sophie, please go into the house,' I said, after hugging her. 'Mummy and Daddy just need a quick chat.'

She looked as if she were going to argue, then went inside. Kevin stared after her; then at me. The dog continued to bark.

'Lorna's been kidnapped,' I said.

Kevin laughed.

'This is your best one yet, Suze. Listen, I don't know if you're hooking up with some guy you met on Tinder or what, but I don't have time for your games. I'm late already. You'll have to tell Sophie that Daddy will see her next weekend; I'm taking her and Lorna to Go Ape.'

'I'm the one who hasn't got time, Kevin,' I said. 'It's true. I got a call from a man who has snatched Lorna. He was telling her to lie down and stop struggling. He has also threatened to drug and kill her unless' – my voice broke – 'I get money to him as soon as I can.'

Silence.

'This is insane,' Kevin said. 'This doesn't happen to people like us; we're not the Kardashians. Let me ring Lorna's mobile.'

I called over my shoulder: 'Just look after Sophie.'

'Suze.' Kevin caught up with me and put a hand on my shoulder. 'If this is real, we have to call the police. Or have the Scouts done that?'

'I don't know, I've not spoken to the Scouts yet. I need to get to the bank.'

Help me, help me.

You will never see her again.

'I'll ring the Scouts,' he said. 'Text me the number.'

I pinged it to him, then opened the car door. I told him that whatever the Scouts said, the police must not be involved.

Help me, help me.

The car park was full so I parked over someone's driveway. Running through the town as it did its business around me, I called Lorna's mobile. No answer.

My phone rang as I was entering the bank. I accepted the call without checking the screen.

'Lorna?'

'Suze, listen.' It was Kevin.

'You need to get off the line in case she calls,' I said. 'Or he does.'

'Suze, it's not true.'

'For God's sake, I heard her voice.'

He was still talking as I approached the desk, behind which a woman with wild blonde hair was surveying her nails. Would she give me such a large amount of money? Would she insist on calling the police if I told her what it was for? I couldn't think, only act.

'I need to make an urgent withdrawal,' I said.

'Suze, stop,' Kevin shouted. 'Listen to me. I rang the Scouts – spoke to a woman called Leanne. Lorna is with them. Leanne – who clearly thought I was mad – told me Lorna was abseiling. She is safe. Do you understand, Suze? Safe.'

'But I spoke to her,' I said. 'She told me to help her. I know her voice, Kevin.'

'She's safe.'

'What if the Scouts are in on it, too? Or what if Leanne didn't really check? What if she was pretending to get you off the phone?'

I'd met Leanne. She seemed nice enough, but was only in her twenties.

'Excuse me,' said a female voice from behind me. 'Do you actually need to speak to the cashier, and if not, can you let me do so?'

'Just a second,' I said to her, and she tutted.

'Suze,' Kevin said. 'I don't know what's going on, but Lorna is fine. Now can you get back so I can get to the match?'

I let the elderly woman behind me speak to the cashier first, while I called the Scouts.

'I spoke to your husband,' Leanne said, in her flat voice, 'sorry, ex-husband. I told him Lorna was fine.'

Was? Shouldn't she have said *is*?

'I know,' I said. 'But I have had phone calls from a man who said he has kidnapped her, and I heard Lorna's voice too. She said she was in danger. And she's not answering her phone.'

'Mrs Watsione,' Leanne said, 'I can see Lorna. She is chatting with a couple of the other Scouts, and they're about to start making dinner. We're encouraging them not to check their phones, that's one of the purposes of the weekend, as you know, to get away from screens and out into nature for its mental health benefits, so that's probably why she's not answering.'

'Leanne, I know this must sound mad. But please, can I speak to Lorna? Otherwise I will have to drive over there, and also call the police.'

'Right,' Leanne said tightly. 'Just a minute, then.'

It was more than a minute; it felt like the longest time of my life. Out of the bank's window, I watched birds landing in trees, surveying the world, then flying away. What freedom to be a bird. I thought of the stories my ornithology-obsessed mother had told me. About pelicans, who people used to think wounded themselves to give their babies their blood, later realising they kept fish in their beaks for them. The partridges, who stole chicks from other birds' nests, although the stolen birds flew back to their mothers when they heard their cries.

'Mum? What's going on? This is seriously weird behaviour. Leanne said you and Dad both called to check I'm okay. That's, like, really embarrassing.'

Tears spilled down my face. This was Lorna. 'Seriously weird behaviour' was what she said all the time. She also often called me embarrassing.

'You're okay, my lovely?' My voice came out as stringy and see-through. 'No strange men have come up to you? No one's scared you?'

'Mum, stop it. You're the one who's scaring me.'

'I know, I'm sorry. I'll explain everything tomorrow,' I said, trying not to sound as though I were crying. 'I love you so much, Lorna. Are you having a good time?'

'Soraya's being weird,' Lorna said, 'but apart from that, yeah, it's okay. Can I go now?'

I repeated that I loved her and ended the call, wiping my eyes.

'Do you need help?' the cashier asked.

'No, sorry.'

As I was going back to the car, thoughts kaleidoscoping, my phone rang again. A private number.

'Where is the money?' demanded the 'kidnapper'. 'If you're not here in half an hour, I will hurt your daughter.'

'I want to speak to her.'

The phone went silent, a vacuum of noise through the glass and plastic. Then: 'Mummy, help me.'

I picked up Sophie and drove us home. While she was playing in her room, I phoned the police. An officer said they couldn't send anyone that day, but someone would be with me in the morning to take a statement.

'This is urgent,' I protested. 'A kidnap threat, as I said. Please, send someone now.'

'We have a large police presence at the football match,' the officer said. 'There is no one available at the moment. Nothing has happened to your daughter, fortunately; it sounds as if you were the intended victim of an AI scam, there's been a few reports of them recently. If you get any more calls from a private number, don't answer.'

'Prank calls?' My voice sounded shrill and fettered. 'This man threatened to kill my daughter. He verbally abused me. How is this not worth taking seriously? He's got my phone number, somehow he's got a recording of her voice... what if he knows my address? I live alone with my eight-year-old daughter.'

'Make sure your windows and doors are locked. Perhaps ask a family member or friend to come round. An officer will be with you tomorrow, between eight thirty and twelve.'

Curled into the sofa like a foetus, I watched the dark growing around me. It was only the need to get Sophie's dinner that made me get up, and I could only manage to make baked beans and sausages for her.

I got two more calls from a private number, and let them go to voicemail. I couldn't bear to listen, but kept them to play to the police.

It was a relief when Sophie went to bed, so I didn't have to pretend to be okay anymore. She had needed an extra-long story time, and then ten minutes of lullabies. Then, when I thought I could get away with leaving her, she asked what had happened to Lorna because she didn't understand. Selecting words like daisies for a chain, linking them delicately so they wouldn't break and I'd have to find more, I told half-truths. Someone had been playing a silly joke but there was no need to worry, Lorna was having fun with her friends and we'd see her tomorrow; it wouldn't happen again; the police would make sure of that. She seemed mostly reassured. I almost told her she could sleep in my bed, but it had taken so long to wean her off doing that I didn't want to set a precedent. If she woke in the night, she could.

I texted Lorna to make sure she was okay, adding a smiley face to soften my obvious paranoia. After an hour, she replied with *Yes*. I gave a heart reaction. My thumb hovered, but I made myself not text again.

As I went downstairs, the loose floorboard on the landing moved beneath my feet and my heart fireworked. I need to numb my feelings, so poured half a bottle of white wine into a glass. Then I double-locked the doors, drew all the curtains and put my phone on silent. It seemed the calls had stopped, but I didn't want to know if there were more.

I put on the TV, for the comfort of the voices, but everything was crime or true crime. How had I watched these programmes, especially the ones about missing children? I found *Seinfeld*, half-watching while googling AI scams, trying to work out what had happened and why I had been targeted. It was usually through social media, I learned; all that was needed was three seconds of audio; voices taken from video clips, dubbed and distorted. Where had he got the audio? Lorna was on Snapchat and Instagram, but I had her passwords and there were no videos of her. Then I remembered the school play she had been in; they had clips on their website. She hadn't said 'Help me' in it, though. And her name wasn't on the site. But then I thought that the man had only said 'Lorna' after I had. I couldn't work out how he had known my own name or phone number, but both were online because of my business and the surname was an unusual one. I'd intended to change it back to my maiden name once Kevin and I were divorced, but had felt sad about having a different name to the girls. I emailed the school with an urgent request to take down the videos. I'd have to work out how we could all be more careful online. From what I could glean, it would have been a real man speaking to me, who presumably would have been there to take my money if I had gone to the industrial estate. What would he have done after that? Then I had a horrible realisation: I'd told him I had an eight-year-old daughter. Had I used Sophie's name? Yes. She was young enough not to have a digital presence, but still.

How could the police regard this as a prank call situation? It was a far cry from my Year Six friends and I finding unusual names in the Phone Book and calling them from our parents' landlines. I had sung Madonna's 'Material Girl' to Mr A. Material. Not nice, but not this.

I was haunted by my daughter's recorded voice. The could-have-been Lorna. It felt as if I'd heard a doppelganger speaking. *It wasn't real*, I told myself. And, *It's over*. The darkness kept asking: *Are you sure?*

I had drunk the glass of wine and was considering whether to pour another, knowing I should go to bed but that sleep would evade me, when the doorbell rang. I froze, heart banging the walls of my chest. Was it him, come for his money?

The bell rang again.

I crept to the kitchen in the dark and picked up the heavy frying pan. Then my phone. This time the police would have to take me seriously.

There were three missed calls. Not from a private number, but from Kevin. Also two texts: *Can you answer the door?*

Don't want to bang and disturb Sophie.

Suze?

Haikus were not my ex's forte.

I was about to open the door, but considered it could be a trick. The 'kidnapper' could have Kevin's number. I rang it.

'I'm outside,' he said, wearily.

'How do I know?'

'Look through the spy-hole, Suze.'

The spy-hole he had installed, when I hadn't liked him working away from home so much. He had done it to soothe my fears, he said. I had been fearing the wrong thing: not what could happen if someone came into the house, but what could happen because of what he was doing outside of it. He had only slept with his colleague Francesca once, he said, but the trust was gone. I had trusted him when he said he'd forsake all others.

'I thought you'd be celebrating the match,' I said, as Kevin followed me into the house. He hadn't been inside for a long time; he usually stood on the doorstep to wait for the girls, even in the winter. He looked around as if he were in a gallery. If he noticed I'd painted the hall a forget-me-not blue, he didn't remark on it.

'I didn't feel much like celebrating,' he said. 'Wanted to check on you and Soph. I was worried when you didn't answer the phone.'

'I didn't want to know if He called again. Didn't feel like being subjected to more threats of my – our – daughter being hurt and killed.'

'Sorry,' he said. 'I should have reacted differently, Suze. If I'd heard what you'd heard, I would have done the same. I've been looking up these scams, it's unbelievable how realistic they are. You were really brave.'

Kindness undid me. As I disintegrated into tears, Kevin made two mugs of tea – I'd moved everything around, but he found everything without needing to ask – which we drank at the breakfast bar. There was a muffling, simplifying reassurance to it.

'How's work?' I said.

'Fine.'

We sank back into silence. It was probably the first time we'd been alone for more than five minutes without the girls since we had split. There seemed too much and not enough to say, like being with someone whose language is rudimentarily known yet with big missing chunks of vocabulary.

'Daddy? Why are you here? Is Lorna hurt?'

It was Sophie, in her guinea pig nightie, hair tousled, holding bunny-in-the-blue-coat to her chest.

'Lorna's not hurt,' I said. 'Daddy came over for a cup of tea; he was passing.'

Sophie hugged him. 'Are you staying the night, Daddy? Please will you?'

'No—' I said.

'I could—' Kevin said at the same time.

JONATHAN WOO

YGGDRASIL CLUB

I

"Yggdrasil Club" was printed on her shirt. I wasn't really looking at her though, just lost in thought at how ridiculous our club T-shirts looked; it was an image of a tree comically stretched with the font looking like it belonged to some kind of table top game. Amina snapped her fingers in front of my face.

"The hell are you staring at?" she asked, taking me out of my daze.

"Nothing, sorry. I think the bus ride drained my energy." I answered. It also didn't help that it was a sweltering 108 degrees outside.

Amina frowned slightly and handed me pamphlets of the museum to pass around.

Now I was *actually* looking at Amina. Her gorgeous, long sun kissed hair swayed as she turned around to pass out the rest of the pamphlets. I almost found myself in another daze just then, but I turned to the group of kids who were waiting on me and yelling about how much they were looking forward to seeing the *sebertoof* bones.

As I was passing them out, I had a proper look at one of them for the first time. There was a drawing of a gigantic elephant creature with equally gigantic looking tusks stuck in some black muck with a sabertooth cat assessing its prey. "Arbrea Tar Pits Museum" was printed on the top. I turned to look at Amina again. She was laughing as she passed her own pile to the group of kids who were making the most amount of ruckus. Her black skater skirt (in which she had tucked in the ridiculous looking T-shirt) made her legs stand out more than usual. She almost turned to me again, but I dissimulated just in time by walking up to the front counter. A lady in a uniform that looked a bit too much like that of an airplane stewardess stood behind a computer monitor.

"These are leftovers," I told her, handing her back a few of the pamphlets. She smiled at me and took them graciously. "That all you folks need?" she asked cheerfully.

"Yeah, thanks again for letting us come in on such short notice. The school just kind of threw all of this at the last minute." I explained to her, not really knowing why. Except maybe to *really* make sure Amina hadn't seen me looking at her.

"No problem at all, we don't get as many elementary school field trip visits as we used to."

I smiled at her tentatively and turned back to where the group of about twenty second grade kids, divided into five groups of four who were playing with the pamphlets, bunching them up or letting them fall to the floor.

Including Amina and myself, there were ten chaperones. Five parents and five students from the "Yggdrasil Club" high school outreach program. I had only joined it because my counselor had told me that I had about ten hours missing from my mandated community service. Without those I could kiss graduation goodbye. So that was how I happened to be at the Arbrea Tar pits on that fateful 108 degree Friday. The day that I had planned to tell Amina how I felt.

As I made my way back to the group, the image of the large elephant and the *sebertoof* came to mind. That dark, obsidian looking muck, bubbling and emitting vapors. My stomach tightened.

II

The tour guide showed up. We made our way through the labyrinthian museum, looking at displays of some bone fragments that were "actually dug up not ten feet from where you stand folks!" which I scoffed at, internally of course. Then we made our way into a portion of the museum that had all its walls painted black to make the illusion of it being night. Some life-like models of strange mammalian creatures I had never seen before were sleeping in a huddle.

While in that room, I caught Amina glancing at me, and I diverted my eyes back to the short woman who was our tour guide.

The mammalian creatures looked like a family of three, the lack of dimorphism in the parent creatures made it impossible to tell who was who. The guide led the group out of the room and I was left there, staring at the child creature.

"You okay, Tim?" Amina said.

I was expecting this to happen. This time I was not surprised by her sudden appearance.

I looked into her light brown eyes, the eyes I had been lost in the moment I walked into the room where the Yggdrasil Club met after school.

"Not really, Amina. There's something I have been meaning to tell you." I told her, looking at the faux stars in the room.

She looked at me with real concern then, an expression I had never seen before.

"What's this about, Tim?" she said, grabbing my hand.

I pulled back my arm as gently as I could.

She furrowed her brow then; my stomach began to turn into a knot again. I could see the black tar, the elephantine creature stuck in it. The *sebertoof,* with its capacious maw.

I took in a deep breath, and looked slightly past her; I couldn't get lost in her eyes.

"I think we should stop seeing each other," I told her firmly.

I could tell she was searching something in my eyes, some kind of bluff. I looked at her face for a second, her brow was no longer furrowed. Instead, a look of apathy adorned her beautiful face.

"You're serious," she said, not asking.

"Yes, you see there's this girl in my bio class—"

"Don't fucking lie to me, Timothy," she said, in a tone I had heard a couple of times.

I winced at that, and then I lost my composure. I looked into her eyes. There was an intensity in them that froze me to my core.

"Why do you have to lie? Why can't you just tell me what's really going on?" she said, crossing her arms.

I wished the ground would swallow me then and there. Not tar, tar would be too slow.

"I—"

"Why'd you even ask me out in the first place anyway?" she asked, taking a step toward me.

I couldn't look her in the eyes anymore. I looked down at my weathered Vans. I felt like a child, being scolded about something real stupid I had done. Maybe this was punishment for trying to force myself into a story that wasn't mine, and Amina was the force of nature responsible for carrying out the punishment.

"Who else is going to take your sorry ass, Tim? Go ahead, tell me who this bio class girl is," she said, taking yet another step closer to me.

I could smell her perfume now. It was a beautiful aroma that I could only describe as a sunny summer Saturday evening. I had become very familiar with that smell, she had worn the very same perfume during our first kiss, behind her apartment complex, hidden away so no one could see us. I could always recall how smooth her lips had been, and how she had softly bitten my lower lip.

She snapped her fingers again at me.

"Who is it?" she asked in a sweeter voice, reaching for my hand again. This time I didn't pull away.

She intertwined her fingers in mine.

ANEETA SUNDARARAJ

SAY HELLO TO YAMA

'Every year, individuals and communities are affected by natural disasters [and] will experience feelings of anxiety, sadness, hopelessness, fatigue, irritability or anger, as well as difficulty sleeping.'

Professor (Adj) Dato' Dr. Andrew Mohanraj

Oh my!

A pewter grey sky with stunning mandarin clouds criss-crossing throughout was more than the necessary drama in what promised to be the tail end of two weeks of floods and the threat of landslides. Squatting behind the village mosque in Kampung Sungai Tua, I looked out at the river. With a single glance, I knew that it was logs of *cengal* that floated downstream. Maybe, the day would come when I'd see His – I refused to say my husband's name; it was best to use pronouns, instead – body floating among the logs.

Because of Him, we ran for our lives.

Because of Him, we lived as one of the hard-core poor.

Because of Him, we'd pretended to be part of a religion we weren't born into.

I stood up and arranged the folds of my kaftan and hijab. Holding the Tupperware containing durians close, I was eager to eavesdrop on the *cakap-cakap* by the water pump. All the way to this gossip session, I lamented as to how my once-charmed life had come to this.

***

The gunpowder grey sky was punctuated by twinkling stars the night He received a phone call from the ah long. The loan shark threatened grievous bodily harm if He didn't settle his debts as soon as possible. A shiny new parang was left outside our front door the next day. Picking up the machete, He shivered upon opening the attached note which read as follows: 'U R Next.'

Within twenty-four hours, we abandoned our lives, boarded the next available bus out of Alor Setar and got off when it stopped outside a mosque in the middle of nowhere. We remained silent when Wahab, the *penghulu* of Kampung Sungai Tua and pseudo-Imam, assuming we were Muslims, saw it as his moral duty to offer us shelter.

"Our sister, Kak Tom, has a small place next to her house. You can stay there."

As we lay on the mat spread out on the floor that first night in our new home, He turned to me and whispered, "Just imagine. From being Ricky, I'm now Ahmad. And you, from Bhoomi, you're now Putri. So easy."

I should have said something, but I didn't know what to say.

I followed Him on his second visit to what the villagers now called 'The Hut'. A forest ranger named Boon Teong explained that it was once a temporary shelter for Rohingya women. They waited for middle men who promised them safe passage to their menfolk in Sumatra and beyond. Instead, they were shipped off to *mamasans* in the city brothels. Once this prostitution and human trafficking ring was busted, the villagers used The Hut as a place to rest whenever they went in search of herbs and other medicinal plants.

"I've got work," He whispered, one day about four months after we'd first arrived. "Some people need to clear the jungle. Use the land to create a latex clone forest farm."

"A what?"

"It's about rubber trees."

"Who said?" Nothing was mentioned about this during the latest *cakap-cakap.*

"Remember Boon Teong? He guessed that I am actually Chinese."

"How?"

"I don't know." He looked at the kettle with boiling water bubbling away.

"This is dangerous."

"No lah." He picked up the *parang* and started to sharpen it. "This will protect us. He wants to help me get extra money to pay off the *ah long* and go home."

"He knows about the *ah long*?" I lifted the kettle off the stove and began to make his *teh tarik.*

"Aiya, no need to think so much, okay?"

He raised his voice. Instinctively, I pulled the ends of my sleeves to hide the fading bruises on my forearm. Had I the courage, I would have asked Him, 'How does that parang help you?'

The day the government changed a year later, supposedly for the better, we had a marbled sky of bright blue with streaks of dull grey. The forest reserve upstream had been cleared. At one thousand metres above sea level, it was what experts called a high hill dipterocarp forest and was deemed environmentally sensitive.

In Kampung Sungai Tua, this called for a gathering – far more serious than the usual *cakap-cakap* – inside the school hall.

Dispensing with preliminaries, Wahab called the meeting to order.

"There are logging activities upstream. Do any of you know anything about this?"

I glanced at Him who was looking straight ahead.

"It's like this," Wahab said. "Put a hen and a few chicks on some grass. Pour a drum of water on them and they will run here, there and everywhere, but the grass will absorb the water. Now, you take away the grass and make it a cement floor. Put the same hen and chicks there. Throw water and what happens? They will be washed away."

Shoulders started to droop.

"What do you think will happen to us when there's heavy rain now? We'll be like those chickens. We will be washed away."

Everyone hung their head low.

Cakap-cakap.

"What happened to the latex clone forest?"

"Not enough money. New company sold the land to an operator of a durian orchard."

"Durian? Our kind of soil, can or not?"

"Sure can. If anything happens, no one will blame us."

"Why, ah?"

"Wahab said because the company got director who is *krabat.* You know lah, with royalty, everything will be okay."

"Ya lah."

The day the trees were completely uprooted for the durian orchard, the sky was ash grey without a single streak of silver. The rays of the sun shone on the spot where a reservoir was created to irrigate the orchard. Reservoir was too posh a word, perhaps, to describe what was nothing more than a gigantic hole in the ground. Soon, previously water-logged plots of flat paddy land were mud-logged testaments that their source of irrigation had become unsuitable for cultivating paddy.

"How could this have happened?"

"Don't ask so many questions, Bhoomi." He opened the leather pouch and counted the notes inside, then sipped on the tumbler of fermented rice called *tuak.*

"This is not good. The Gods will be angry. Then how? Yama will come."

"You and your Yama. No need to bring all this Hindu-Bindu gods." Shivering, he showed his disgust for my faith by adding, "Eeee...."

I looked away. Something wasn't right. I could feel it. It was also the moment when I first had an inkling that there would come a time when I would need to gather my wits about me.

Life bumbled along until the day I couldn't see the sky through the fat raindrops. As the twilight hour began, He rushed into our space.

"I saw him, Bhoomi."

"Who?"

"Him." When I stared, perplexed, He shook his hands in front of him, frustrated. "The *ah long.*"

"W-h-a-?" I cleared my throat.

"Boon Teong brought him to the durian orchard. This *ah long* fellow is his friend lah! Die-die, I tell you."

As I watched Him gather his things into a plastic bag – one shirt, a pair of trousers, phone charger and toiletries – it dawned on me. He was packing for one.

"What about me?"

He stopped, stood up and held my shoulders.

"I will go first. Pay this *ah long* fellow." Suddenly, He started hitting his head with his palm. "Alamak! I forgot the pouch." He began pacing. "It's in The Hut. I go back there to get money." One more squeeze of my shoulders and he added, "But I will leave some money there for you. Five hundred ringgit."

The next thing I knew, He was gone.

I stood there, in the middle of our one hundred square feet dwelling place for the past five years, accepting my reality for the first time ever. I had married a self-centred, good-for-nothing who didn't care if I lived or died.

The fading inky blue sky didn't help to light my path to The Hut. If it had, I could have been forewarned. As it transpired, it was Boon Teong's left hand I saw first when I stepped into The Hut. It was minus the ring finger. It seemed, He said months ago, Boon Teong had lost it at an irritated goldsmith's shop.

The next thing I saw was the leather pouch.

"Ah, there you are. There is a lot of money here. Five thousand lah. That Ricky made a lot, ah?"

For a long while, I watched him.

"Please, give me my money. My husband's money."

"Your husband?" He sniggered. "My friend saw him the other day. My friend, ah, not so kind one, you know. And money still here, what? Maybe… you know."

I held my breath.

"Now, all alone." We made eye contact then. A brief encounter – one that left me certain of what he was implying.

I tried to grab the pouch from him.

"Ah, ah, ah," the Boon Teong deflected. "Tell you what. Here," he said, handing the pouch to me. "Take it."

He did not let go, though, when I put my hand on the pouch.

"I want something in return."

I should have let go of the pouch then. But I needed the money.

When I couldn't admit to myself what happened next, how was anyone going to believe a word I said?

"Ah," Boon Teong said when it was over. "Here. Five hundred ringgit. I will keep the rest. Keep safe for you." Zipping his pants, he said, "Come back next Wednesday, okay?"

With each step back down the hill, I recited a mantra to the spirits watching and begged for forgiveness for defiling their space.

"Ah," Boon Teong said when it was over. "Here. Five hundred ringgit. I will keep the rest. Keep safe for you." Zipping his pants, he said, "Come back next Wednesday, okay?"

With each step back down the hill, I recited a mantra to the spirits watching and begged for forgiveness for defiling their space.

A thousand curses unto Him. He'd taken the *parang* with Him and I had nothing but my wits to defend myself. I heard the rumble and opened my eyes.

Peeping through the gaps in wood, the sky was a canopy of velvety black. Turning my back to the apology for a door hanging off its hinges, I opened the pill box and dropped the tablets into the plastic bottle of fermented rice wine. Watching the effervescence, I prayed that the three hundred ringgit I'd paid for the pills be worth every sen. The faith healer promised that three pills were enough to knock out an elephant.

I heard their words.

"How much? Hundred?"

"No lah. No need so much. Fifty each enough. This orang kampung only. Give this durian also enough already."

The bastard meant to short change me. There was only one thing to do. I slipped all the pills into the jug making it three pills each for three lecherous souls. I flung open the door. Boon Teong turned, saw me holding out the jug and three tumblers. Greedy, they drank every drop and fell face down into the mud.

***

Cakap-cakap.

"Putri, you heard or not, what happened?"

"What?"

"Two Chinaman. One Malay fellow. Died lah."

"Oh."

"Wahab found them near The Hut. But all hush-hush because the Malay fellow is *krabat."*

"Oh… You want? Durian?"

"Wah! Delicious."

Under the fading dawn sky, chequered shades of pale yellow and powder blue, I squatted next to the logs by the river. I pulled the pouch from its hiding place and put it into the plastic bag I brought back from *cakap-cakap,* I stood up. At that very moment, a body floated past. It was bloated, caked in mud, hands akimbo and fingers splayed. The ring finger on the right hand was missing.

"Say Hello to Yama."

First published in *Livina Press* (Spring 2023), shortlisted for Aesthetica's International Creative Writing Award 2024 (December 2023) and included in a collection of short stories by the author called *Tapestry of the Mind* (Penguin Random House SEA, 2024).

JON FAIN

PROBABLY A NAME FOR IT

The overwhelming smell wasn't the traditional one. With only the two sisters and their families this year, there was no need for a kid's table. Instead adults and children alternated. But counting it up, a place-setting short. Where was her husband?

The wine they'd brought never made it to the meal. He considered the missing husband, his brother-in-law by some definition. Men married to sisters, there was probably a name for it. His not being there a surprise, but less so than the newly red walls, matching the paint on his sister-in-law's thin wrists. He sat next to his nephew, the youngest and only boy among the cousins, dished out his food, cut up his meat. A fat kid, quiet unlike his Dad. Trying to impress him the reason for the expensive wine. No doubt the reason it had been whisked away.

On the way out, he tried to find the bottle in the refrigerator crowded with plastic tubs and tin-foiled turkey. On the drive home, they argued while the twin girls slept in back. Your sister has been through a lot, he said, remembering her moving from the kitchen in her loose pale green dress and her paisley head-scarf, to the head of the table. He couldn't get around her being that sick. No symptoms at all—but then the harsh pronouncement after a routine exam, treatments looming like a bully waiting after school. He decided he was okay with the missing thirty dollar Riesling. The turkey was dry, pre-cooked. Without giblets it came to table without gravy. If I'd known, his wife said, I would have brought some. But then I suppose that would have disappeared too.

Her sister's troubles had always trumped hers. She'd hadn't had it easy either, she reminded him later, in the dark. He'd fantasized about sex with his sister-in-law countless times. In spite of the illness and rigor of the possible cure she still looked good, although hadn't worn the perfume he liked. At dawn the next morning, his turn for the dog, pulling on his pants and new sweater bought especially for the holiday, it came back—no turkey cooking, instead that fresh thick paint smell, still in his clothes. Walling them in with her, brick red.

First published in *(mac)ro(mic)* in June 2020

GOOD AULD JIMMY

Auld Jimmy trudged up the seventy-two steps to his third floor flat on Leith Walk. It was hard going for a pensioner. He met the busybody wifey from Number 7 on the second landing.

"I haven't seen you in ages, Jimmy. How are things?"

"All right, I suppose." He leaned on the banister to catch his breath.

"And how's the wee kitty?"

"Same as ever."

"Isn't it cruel keeping the animal cooped up inside," she said, chin in the air, emphasis on *cruel*. "Cats like to roam."

"Roger has everything he needs."

"Has he had all his shots? Cat flu can be very serious."

"That's all sorted," said Jimmy, and he continued up the stairs.

Bloody nosey woman. He didn't have money to spend on vets. It was hard enough making ends meet on a pittance of a pension.

Roger pitter-pattered into the hallway, as Jimmy locked the door.

"How do you fancy a trip to the vet?" He bent down to rub the cat's head. "And have your furry arse jabbed with needles."

Jimmy didn't expect an answer from the orange tabby. He wasn't one of those numpties who believed cats were human.

He put his shopping bag on the oak table in the kitchen. It was the first piece of furniture he bought after getting married, and he could account for every nick and scorch mark. Two years a widower, Jimmy missed his Sally but he didn't feel lonely. He had his routine, and he had Roger.

Jimmy took off his outside shoes, put on his slippers, and went into the front room. Roger sat on the window sill, observing the Edinburgh traffic. He had been Sally's cat—she got him as a kitten from a cousin. Jimmy often felt that a part of her remained with him in Roger.

Seeing Roger perched so prim and proper, Jimmy had to wrap him in his arms and squeeze him tight. He liked the feel of the cat's sleek fur, the meatiness of the haunches and hardness of the ribs. If he pressed hard enough, Jimmy fancied he could feel the cat's liver and kidneys and heart.

"You're a great wee puss."

When he put Roger down, the sleeves of his jumper were covered in fur.

He got the old comb from the dresser, and started brushing the cat. Roger treated it as a game, rolling on his back and batting Jimmy's hand.

"Come on you minx, how about some cooperation?"

He grabbed the cat's back leg, amused by the look of annoyance on Roger's face. The comb stuck in the fur, Roger hissed and Jimmy gave him a sharp smack on the nose.

"Do that again, and you'll be sorry."

It was time for supper. Jimmy didn't see any point buying cat food. Roger ate what he ate, mackerel or else chicken or meat pie. Once a week, Jimmy cooked up his specialty; fried minced beef, bacon and peas, seasoned with pepper and a dash of Worcester sauce.

He poured water from the tap into a dish, and Roger lapped it with his spiny tongue. No milk, not after the liquid shite the cat had left in the litter tray for Jimmy to deal with.

Supper over, Jimmy washed his cup and plate in the sink. He never used the dishwasher. It was coming up to eight o'clock, the evening unremitting in its emptiness. Nothing on television but talk shows and the costume dramas Sally had liked so much. Jimmy preferred documentaries; hard facts about real life.

Roger lay curled up, asleep on the recliner. Jimmy tossed him onto the floor. In his home his rules applied, and the recliner was for watching television. Later, he let the cat jump up beside him. Roger made himself comfortable, paws folded, eyes opening slowly and closing. Jimmy scratched the cat's dainty chin, and felt the deep vibrating *purr*.

Routine was important to Jimmy, something Sally had never properly appreciated. He got up every morning at seven thirty. First thing, a cup of tea and a shave, then out to get *The Scotsman* from the Tesco Express across the road. A bowl of porridge for breakfast, the same for Roger. Jimmy read the newspaper over a second cup of tea—sports results first, then the news section, leaving the obituaries for last.

He took care with his appearance, had his hair cut on the first Monday of the month, and never went out without a shirt and tie. Even so, Jimmy looked his age with his old man's hands, wrinkles and turkey neck. Five foot eight in his socks and a little stooped, maybe no longer so nimble but he could fit into the suit he'd worn as a much younger man.

He got out of the flat by two o'clock. A jaunt around Pilrig Park, then down to Leith docks to check on the ships. Jimmy kept his eyes on the ground, no interest in the shop windows or the people he passed. He rarely thought about his time as a lab technician in the university, and hadn't kept in touch with anyone from work. That part of his life had ended. Jimmy didn't expect kindness from others. He was beholden to nobody.

Most Saturdays, he walked the length of Princes Street Gardens, stopping to view statues of important men the likes of David Livingstone and Allan Ramsay. He always sat on the bench across from The Ross Fountain. It had an inscription on a brass plate that read: *Craig Gallbraith, 16/3/1953-28/4/1979. Did you get what you wanted?* Gallbraith was born the same year as Jimmy.

He watched the passersby gaping at their phones, and almost walking into each other. Obsessed with themselves, like the university students. In all his time in the teaching labs, Jimmy never received a word of thanks, no appreciation for the help he'd given them to get their degrees.

He went to The Iona Bar on Monday, Wednesday and Friday afternoons, availing of the oldies' *nip and wee nip* deal. They all knew about Roger in The Iona.

"You should see the way the cat grooms himself," he told them. "Every inch of fur, from behind the ears to a thorough washing of his arse."

"You sure like your cat, Jimmy," Davy, the barman, said.

"Is he right pawed or left pawed?" one regular wanted to know.

"What do you mean?" Jimmy asked.

"Your cat, does he favour his right or left paw?"

Jimmy thought about it. "Left."

"He's not a typical tabby then."

"Don't I know it."

Early in April, Jimmy received a letter about his pension. He hated anything to do with paperwork. Sally had looked after that side of things. This was a final reminder and, if he didn't act, he wouldn't get his payment that month.

Sitting at the table, he went through the instructions and filled in the form until he got to the section requiring proof of identity. He was Jimmy McIver, and had been Jimmy McIver for sixty-nine years.

Roger sidled into the kitchen, sat and stared at him.

"Bloody bureaucracy. You don't appreciate how easy you've got it. A full belly, and no worries."

It stated in the instructions that proof of identity could be provided by a signature from a doctor or priest or bank official. Wanting nothing to do with the first two, he'd have to go to the bank.

He put on his good Crombie coat and cashmere scarf, and set off for the branch on Shandwick Place. Up Leith Walk, onto Princes Street and through the gardens. He stopped for a breather at Adam Black's statue, and sat for a few minutes on Craig Galbraith's bench.

It had been years since he'd been in a bank. He always used the ATM beside the Tesco Express to take out money. The bank was empty, nobody queuing and nowhere to queue. No counters or cashiers, just wee computers on glass tables.

A lassie caked in make-up came up to him.

"Can I help you, sir?" she asked, talking to him like he was a doddery fool who didn't belong in this shiny new world.

Jimmy adjusted the sleeves of his Crombie, and straightened his scarf. He was no backward fogey,
whining about machines replacing people. Jimmy understood technology.

"I need a document certified," he said. "It's for my pension," he added, which made him sound weak and helpless.

"Let me check with my colleague."

She was replaced by a pudgy guy in a suit, hair arranged to cover a bald spot.

"I understand you need a document certified," he said, all smiles and authority.

"That's right," Jimmy replied, looking around. So, he wasn't going to get the courtesy of sitting in an office. "Can you do that for me? It just needs a stamp or a signature."

"No problem. There'll be a twenty pound fee."

"What do you mean?" Jimmy felt rage erupt in his belly, rage at being left standing like a beggar and treated like a fool. "I've had an account in this bank for forty years, and you're charging me for a signature."

"It's the bank's policy."

Jimmy didn't stop in The Iona on his way home. Twenty pounds poorer, ripped off by his own bank. He'd have liked to punch that baldy bawbag, but what could he do but pay up.

He dragged himself up the seventy-two steps. Roger wasn't waiting in the hallway. He found the cat in the bedroom, sprawled on the bed. Roger stretched and yawned. Jimmy grabbed the duvet and pulled it over the cat. Pressing down, he felt the animal wriggle, and sensed its panic. Roger let out a plaintive cry. Jimmy pressed harder. He stepped away from the bed, releasing a flurry of movement under the duvet. The cat sprang off the bed, streaked across the room, crashing against the bedroom door, and out of sight.

He shouldn't lose control like that, but the cat wasn't blameless. What good was it? What real help was it to Jimmy? He was stuck with the thing—Sally's bloody cat. A burden, all it did was eat, sleep and shit, and create a mess for him to clean.

At suppertime, Roger reappeared, attracted by the sound of Jimmy banging the food bowl with a spoon. The cat backed away as he approached, eyes blinking when he bent down and offered his hand. Jimmy heated some meat pie, and gave Roger a little extra.

The following Friday, he was back in The Iona. Angus sat beside him. A better class of customer, silver-haired and always well turned out in a blazer with a handkerchief in the breast pocket. They discussed the relative merits of cats and dogs.

"Dogs show blind allegiance to their owners," Angus said. "But you can't expect that from a cat. They're independent animals who'll accept food if it's offered and accommodation if it's convenient. Anything else is a bonus."

Angus was well-read, and needed little encouragement to display his erudition.

"Behind every great writer, you'll find a cat," he said. "Hemingway's five-toed cats, Céline's brave Bébert and Dickens' gentle Wilhelmena. Cats are philosophers, dogs are not philosophers."

Not the usual pub blather, and better than griping about the weather or football.

"You're a scientist, Jimmy," Angus said. "So you'll appreciate Macak, the cat who educated Tesla about electricity. And Newton's cat, Spithead, who invented the cat flap."

Whenever Jimmy offered to buy a drink, Angus accepted but never returned the favour.

"Everyone knows about Laika, the dog. But what about Félicette, the first cat in space."

"I didn't know that," Jimmy said.

"And we shouldn't forget Franz Helm's rocket cats."

Whatever Angus had to say about cats being philosophers and inventors, Jimmy sometimes thought he'd be better off with a dog. At least, you'd get some gratitude from a dog. You could take a dog for a walk, and bring him into the pub. Having a dog with you would break the ice, a good way to start a conversation. Greeting other dog walkers in Pilrig Park, maybe stopping to chat, pass a minute or two, nothing more. No need to get pally, no reason to be beholden to them.

Summer was well advanced, the flat stuffy even with the windows open. Back from buying *The Scotsman*, Jimmy noticed something wrong with Roger. His posture wasn't right, hunched and pathetic, staring at his food without eating.

That evening, there was no sign of the cat. Jimmy searched high and low, and eventually found him under the bed.

"What are you doing there?"

With Jimmy's coaxing, Roger crawled out from his hiding place. The cat's nose was dry, and rough like sandpaper. One side of his face appeared swollen. Gently rubbing his ears triggered weak purring.

Roger made a pathetic attempt to nuzzle against Jimmy.

He didn't know what to do. Should he take the cat to a vet? He dithered, and decided to wait another day. Whatever about the cost, he didn't want outsiders involved, not yet.

Sticking to his routine, he went for a nip and wee nip in The Iona. He said nothing about Roger. Angus waved to him from the bar. Jimmy left, avoiding having to talk to him.

Back in the flat, Jimmy fixed a loose hinge on a cabinet, washed the dishes, and paced the hall. Roger sat on the recliner, mouth open, and body trembling with each breath. The poor wee thing, so delicate and helpless.

Jimmy lay awake that night. What would he do without Roger? It had happened so quickly, without any warning. Only days ago, Roger had been playing with a paperclip, making a terrible racket. Jimmy regretted his irritation, and the way he'd shouted at the cat.

The next day, Roger seemed better, his breathing more regular but he was still not eating. Jimmy lifted him carefully, cradling him in his arms. The swelling had gone down.

Later, Roger lapped the water in his bowl, and picked at a piece of mackerel. Definite signs of recovery—maybe there'd be no need for a vet.

The following morning, Jimmy experienced a surge of relief, hearing the cat digging in the litter. Roger ate a full bowl of porridge. The worst had passed, and everything could return to normal.

In The Iona, Jimmy explained how great a responsibility it was to keep a cat.

"The wee thing is dependent on me. I've nothing to gain from the cat. I feed it instead of letting it starve. It's what makes us different from animals."

"That's one lucky cat," Davy said. "Maybe I'll move in, and you can look after me."

They liked Jimmy in The Iona. Good auld Jimmy, always ready to put his hand in his pocket and buy a round.

Every so often, whenever he remembered, Jimmy watered the spider plants on the dresser. Sally had filled the flat with houseplants. The spider plants were all that had survived, the flower boxes on the back windows long gone to seed.

He noticed scratch marks on the side of the dresser, and shavings on the ground. The bloody cat had started tearing the furniture again. Jimmy was sure he'd put a stop to that.

Not for the first time, as he spooned out the porridge, Roger butted his head against the spoon, spilling a glob on the ground.

"Eat that." Jimmy pointed to the spilt porridge.

The cat looked in a different direction.

"Do you understand anything I say?"

Jimmy grabbed Roger, and stuck his nose in the porridge. Roger shook his head, backing away from the bowl.

"Come back here."

The cat ignored Jimmy, and walked away. Jimmy moved quickly, grabbed

Roger and lifted him by the skin of the neck. The cat hung in the air, legs dangling.

"You never listen, do you? Never obey anything. Scratching the dresser, you little fucker."

Jimmy dropped the cat, and Roger scrambled away, claws tearing at the linoleum to gain purchase.

After breakfast, Jimmy watched Roger slinking around the front room. He hunkered down, and enticed the cat over.

"Come here, no need to go into a sulk."

He took Roger in his arms, gripped his legs and pulled him closer.

"You're a great wee puss." He rested his chin on the cat's head, feeling the flicker of Roger's ears against his cheek.

Jimmy went to the pet section of the Tesco Express, taking his time to choose a cat toy. In the end, he opted for a feathery thing on a long stick.

In the flat, Roger chased the toy as Jimmy pulled it behind him, going from the kitchen, through the hall and into the front room. Nine or ten years old, Roger wasn't showing his age, leaping from floor to chair to couch in rapid jumps.

"You're too quick for me."

Ten years, Jimmy thought, must be old for a cat. With Sally gone, how much time did he have left with Roger?

The nosey wifey from downstairs showed up, claiming she'd heard loud mewing through the air vents.

"Is the kitty all right? Such terrible crying, the poor thing sounded in pain."

Jimmy had to let her in, and she cooed over Roger who paid her no attention.

"Such a cute kitty," she said.

Roger yawned, and sniffed the air.

"Aren't cats mysterious creatures?"

"They are, I suppose." Jimmy walked her to the door.

After she left, Jimmy played with Roger, pulled his tail and rubbed his belly as the cat kicked his back paws. A flash of claws drew blood on Jimmy's wrist, putting an end to the game.

On a damp Wednesday evening in November, Jimmy came in from The Iona, and hung his coat on the hook in the hallway. He checked his wallet; only five pounds left. He'd bought that windbag Angus a drink, and had to listen to more patter about five-toed cats and rocket cats. Drinks for two other chancers at the bar in return for their good auld Jimmy shite. He was an easy touch, an auld fool.

He heard noises in the kitchen. Roger lay, spread out, pawing at something under the fridge. The cat jumped up, stood on his back legs, then pounced and slid on the floor, knocking a piece of dry spaghetti against the wall. The stupid bloody cat. Jimmy had boiled up pasta to go with his mince dish the night before. Roger caught the spaghetti in his claws and tossed it in the air, playful and destructive.

"You little fucker."

Jimmy held him by the tail, and pulled him off the floor. He squeezed the cat, enfolding him in his arms. Roger struggled to escape, squirming and mewling. Jimmy flung the cat away. Roger fell on his side, regained his balance and looked up at Jimmy with terrible, questioning yellow-green eyes before scampering into the hall. Jimmy stood at the sink, his fists clenched.

The cat would return in his own time, but Jimmy felt too much remorse. He went to find Roger and console him, guilty but also irked for allowing the cat to gain the upper hand. Just like Sally, passive but always goading him, never offering any support.

Soon, he had Roger sitting on his lap. Auld Jimmy caressed the soft fur, his fingers probing deeper, feeling the cat's ribs.

"You're a great wee puss."

SHORESIDE

For years, I had longed to return to Shoreside. The memories of it from my childhood were strong yet somehow incomplete. I remembered the long walk along the wooden boardwalk that connected the town to the beach at the lake's edge, walking across wet pebble-strewn ground covered by a shallow layer of water that ran alongside the wooden support beams of the boardwalk teasing the nearness of the lake just ahead. I had jumped down three feet to the ground to walk barefoot over the wet pebbles to cool my feet from the hot planks we had been walking on and relieve my bored impatience. I remembered the old, quaint buildings of the small town, brick with white wood siding on the upper floors. (It was more of a village, really). It looked untouched since the 1800s, with many buildings containing a hotel, a cafe, restaurants, drinking establishments, or small gift shops that sold interesting or unique items such as handmade toys and souvenirs for visiting tourists. Somewhere in a box of childhood things was a small, carved wooden lighthouse I'd purchased there from a shop, the only time my father and I visited the place. I vividly remembered visiting the marshes close to the lake and wading through the marsh-grass as waves lapped at my ankles and frogs and birds peeped around me while my father sat in a chair on a nearby dock, watching me chase minnows in the shallow water. I often asked my father when we could return to Shoreside to visit again, and he said, "Someday, maybe. We'll see." I clearly remembered all of these things. What I did not remember was visiting the shore of the lake, which inspired the name of Shoreside, or seeing the lighthouse I had purchased a replica of so many years ago. I had no idea what lake the town bordered or what state the town that we had visited was located in. My father passed away ten years ago, so I could not ask him.

After countless dead-end internet searches, I found the town again. I turned up pictures of the cluster of buildings connected by a long boardwalk, a rocky, tan stretch of sand by a lake, and a photo of the familiar lighthouse perched on a tiny island far out in the lake. None of these, except the town's buildings, stirred any familiar memories of my visit.

With a two-month break from work looming ahead of me, I resolved to take the long drive to Shoreside to revisit the town and experience what it had to offer as an adult, hoping to fill in the missing pieces of my childhood memories. I convinced my wife Claire that a road trip would be fun and give us time to relax on a beach in a picturesque old town, recounting my childhood visit and my desire to visit again. After tracking down the number for the Shoreside Hotel, I called, even though I was confident they would have no vacancies, as this was probably the height of the tourist season. I expected to call multiple hotels in the surrounding area to locate a room. To my surprise, the woman who answered, who was also the hotel's owner, picked up immediately and politely explained that they had plenty of rooms, asked our preferences, and put us down for a reservation without requesting a credit card or a deposit. I considered it fortunate timing and thought nothing more of it.

After a lengthy drive, we entered the town through a viaduct beneath a raised train passage, a ridge of earth that I presumed also formed a sort of levee to keep the chance of flooding from the lake from occurring. After passing through, the little town lay directly ahead of us. A wide lane of pebbled surface formed the main street through the place. It was flanked on one side by a row of white brick buildings connected by a wooden plank boardwalk instead of a sidewalk. The other side held a few Victorian-looking houses stretching out into the distance. The effect was quaint and striking. Claire and I admired the view for a moment before turning and parking in the lot that lay along the raised levee/train passage before getting out to stretch our legs and determine which of the brick buildings housed the hotel that we were to be staying at.

The hotel was easy to find, the only three-story building of all the buildings along the boardwalk. After checking in and being shown to our small, quaint room, we donned our shorts and swimwear and decided to walk to the beach and enjoy the rest of the afternoon. I asked the woman at the check-in desk, who appeared to be the owner I spoke to previously, the best way to the beach. She got a strange look on her face, a small tight smile, and a slight furrowing of the skin between her eyebrows and said to me in return, "I take it that this is your first visit to Shoreside?" I replied that I had visited once in my childhood, probably at eight or nine, and had always meant to return and visit since then. She said, "Go out the front doors, follow the boardwalk to the left, and keep going until it ends." She also suggested that we should, "Check out the various shops along the way. There's a good restaurant-bar where the boardwalk widens and veers to the right."

We stepped out into bright sunshine and the soft sound of water rolling across the pebbled street, under and to the right of the raised boardwalk. The temperature was hot but bearable, with a nice breeze blowing gently along the planked walk, probably from the lake ahead. We continued walking, glancing into the storefront windows as we passed, shop owners sitting outside the open doors of their establishments on wooden chairs, or on the benches that lined that side of the walk, or waving cheerily to us from inside through the plate glass front windows as they arranged their displays. The whole vibe was peaceful, cheery, and very homey.

Upon reaching the outside dining deck for the restaurant, we stopped and sat at one of the umbrella-shaded tables, and ordered two beers with a basket of fries to enjoy while we took a break from the sun and the walk. The boardwalk stretched out before us, promising a still longer walk ahead. As I shoved a delicious home fry into my mouth and chased it with a swallow of cold beer, I noticed that along the rail was placed a beach umbrella, an empty cooler, and a couple of beach towels draped across the rail. I gestured to our server, a young man in his early twenties, and pointed out that one of their patrons had inadvertently left their beach equipment behind.

"Oh yeah," he replied. "That happens all the time. That stuff has been sitting there for days now."

"They didn't come back looking for it?" I asked.

"Nope," he replied, offering no further explanation.

"That's weird," I said to Claire, and looked across the broad, pebbled Main Street of town. I began to visually inspect the picturesque, well-maintained houses that lined that side of the street. Further down in the direction of the lake, one stood out both for its size (having a sizeable atrium-like structure attached to its side with skylights and two walls composed of floor-to-ceiling windows) and for a large sign across the front reading, 'The Marshes at Shoreside.'

Curious, I suggested to Claire that we walk over and check it out when we finished our snack. After downing the last swallow of my beer, we left a generous tip and, going down a short set of stairs that led to ground level, walked across the pebbled Main Street with its surface covered by an inch or so of water, which rippled away towards the direction that the lake, still out of view, lay. The water felt cool and refreshing as it lapped through our sandals. Mounting the front steps, we could see a sign in the front door's glass reading, 'COME IN, WE'RE OPEN.' Turning the handle and hesitantly opening the door, we found ourselves standing in the large front room of a home decorated in a Victorian style, which hinted that this was once the front parlor meant to welcome visiting guests. At the far end of the room sat a desk with an elderly man seated behind it, who welcomed us and asked if we were there to visit the exhibit. I explained that we were tourists in town and were walking around to check out places of interest. "Well, you've come to the right place," he said. "I think that you'll find our exhibit very interesting."

"What is it exactly?" I inquired. "Outside, it says the Marshes at Shoreside."

"And that's just what it is," he said, smiling. "An exact replica of the Shoreside Marshes, recreated to the best of my ability. I spent hours and hours there as a child and wanted to recreate it for guests visiting the town. Entry is five dollars, but I think you will be pleased with the value of the exhibit. I'd also be happy to answer any questions about the history of Shoreside. I was born and raised here and have lived here all my life. I'm also the town's mayor—not to brag too much."

I smiled at him, thanked him, and handed him a ten-dollar bill.

"Right through this door," he said, gesturing to the door situated next to the desk. "Welcome to the marshes."

I turned the handle and opened the door to a surprising sight. Claire and I found ourselves standing on a wooden dock above a pool of water, with low waves rippling across its surface, and marsh grass rising in patches everywhere, as small fish swam among it, above the sand and stone-covered bottom. The sounds of frogs and water birds echoed over the quiet, peaceful scene, seemingly from speakers mounted high around the room. The far wall held a mural of a lake stretching into the distance, and a tall, old-fashioned lighthouse stood on a small island just offshore. As Claire sat down in one of the wooden loungers along the dock, she sighed. She said, "It's beautiful. So peaceful."

I slipped off my sandals and sat on the dock's edge, dangling my feet into the water below. The recreation was remarkable, identical in every way to my childhood memories of the place. I considered hopping down into the water to wade among the grasses and reeds, as I had done as a child, until I spotted the notice posted up high, 'NO ENTRY INTO WATER.' That was disappointing, as the water was not much more than a foot deep. Still, I could understand the safety concerns for small children who might damage the exhibit or drown, so instead, I slipped on my sandals after wiping the water from my feet and went through the door to ask the older man more about the natural marshes.

"It's a beautiful exhibit," I said, as I entered the room and faced him. "Just like I remember Shoreside. I wonder if I might ask you a few questions about the marshes and the lake."

"I'll answer whatever I can for you, young man."

"Can you give me directions to find the real marshes? They're obviously along the shore of the lake, some- where, but is there a specific trail that leads there?"

"No, son, I'm afraid you're about sixty years too late for that visit."

"I don't understand; I visited them when I was eight or nine. My dad took me."

"Then you must be as old as me," he said. "I have to say that you look great for seventy-five. You don't look a day over forty."

"But, I remember playing there. Waves splashing, chasing minnows as my dad sat on the do…" I opened the door again and looked inside. Claire was sitting on the dock in the lounge chair. The marsh frogs were peeping, as an owl hooted in the distance. Here was the place I visited. The one in my memory. No wonder it seemed so eerily accurate. I stepped back, closed the door, and turned again to the elderly proprietor.

"You're right. It was here that I visited."

"Glad you have fond memories of the place. We don't get a lot of return visitors anymore."

"What happened to the marshes?"

"Drained away, just like the lake."

"What do you mean? I'm confused."

"I can understand why. It's a long, sad story, but I'm willing to tell it if you're willing to listen."

"Please do," I said as Claire entered through the door beside me. She walked and stood behind me, resting her hand on my shoulder as I stood listening, hands in my pockets.

"Where would you like me to start? From the beginning is probably best."

"We're all ears," I said, reaching up to place my hand on the one Claire had resting on my shoulder.

"The town was founded in 1927 by a man named Archibald Shore. He had the idea to create a resort town with the feel of his home on the Atlantic coast. He funded the lake's creation in the valley between the mountains and then built the town to look like an old New England one. He built it up-ground in a valley section in expectation of the lake filling over the years and rising to

BIOGRAPHIES

KAREN PIERCE GONZALEZ'S poetry collections include *True North, Coyote in the Basket of My Ribs and Sightings from a Star Wheel.* Forthcoming: *Down River with Li Po.* An award-winning writer and artist, her work has appeared in numerous publications. She lives in the North San Francisco Bay Area. Twitter (X) @folkheartpress

ELLIE SNYDER is a poet from Montana, now living next door in Boise, Idaho. She writes and manages socials for a nonprofit helping people, pets and the planet. Read her work in *The Blood Pudding, Fauxmoir, Pinky Thinker Press, In Parentheses* and elsewhere, and find her on Twitter @egsnyds

O.E.L is a twenty-two year old graduate student studying social work in Chicago, Illinois. She has been previously published by *Ghost City Press,* and shares her work mainly via social media. O.E.L reads and writes both poetry and fiction in her own time, and is inspired heavily by introspective and metaphoric language.

NICK CROMWELL is a writer in the Pacific Northwest who is currently working on his first novel and has written countless poems and letters. He can be found on Instagram @cromwell.nick

SERAPHINE SAINTCLAIR is primarily a poet, singer/songwriter and photographer but she enjoys creating in other mediums as well. In her work she especially loves to explore the worlds of her emotions and the mystical. She has been published in *The Winged Moon Magazine* and has self-published six books of poetry. She is working on new poetry collections, as well as an album of music, a novel, and multiple projects involving her photography. On Tumblr she is @ seraphinesaintclair

DESTINY RITCHIE is an upcoming poet from a very small town in West Virginia. She writes about experiences to share and connect with others. What's not written in her upcoming book, *Steep Hills and Sharp Curves,* can be found on Twitter (X) @KumirAgne

THOMAS DIMASSIMO is an Italian-American writer from Atlanta, GA. In addition to his late night Tumblr musings, Thomas also works as a screen and television writer. He does not recommend you ever order anything called 'disco fries.'

JOHNNY CARAMAC is a man late in years, a drifter that finally settled. A baker of Bread, who loves to play with words and maybe emotions. He is a soulless man with an empty grin. He is now to be found in the East Midlands of England.

BERNARD PEARSON's work appears in over one hundred publications worldwide including *Aesthetica Magazine, The Edinburgh Review, and The York Literary Review.* In 2017, a selection of his poetry *In Free Fall* was published by Leaf Press. In 2019, he won second prize in The Aurora Prize for Writing for his poem *Manor Farm.*

JOHN GREY is an Australian poet, US resident, recently published in N*ew World Writing, North Dakota Quarterly and Lost Pilots.* His latest books, *Between Two Fires, Covert* and *Memory Outside The Head* are available through Amazon. His work is upcoming in *California Quarterly, Seventh Quarry, La Presa and Doubly Mad.*

ANDREW BUCKNER is a multi award-winning filmmaker and screenwriter. A noted poet, critic, author, actor, and experimental musician, he runs and writes for the review site AWordofDreams.com. He is on Twitter at Moviesforlife09

KUSHAL PODDAR is the author of Postmarked Quarantine and has eight books to his credit. He is a journalist, father, and the editor of Words Surfacing. His works have been translated into twelve languages and published across the globe. Twitter: Kushalpoe

MICK MALONE is an artist and author from Pittsburgh, PA. He has released five collections of poetry and artwork, and several zines. He has never died. His artwork can be viewed on Instagram @gravebug and his writing can be read on Tumblr @MickMalone

ALEX CARRIGAN (he/him) is a Pushcart-nominated editor, poet, and critic from Alexandria, VA. He is the author of *Now Let's Get Brunch: A Collection of Ru-*

Paul's Drag Race Twitter Poetry (Querencia Press, 2023) and *May All Our Pain Be Champagne: A Collection of Real Housewives Twitter Poetry* (Alien Buddha Press, 2022). He has appeared in *The Broadkill Review, Sage Cigarettes, Barrelhouse, Fifth Wheel Press, Cutbow Quarterly,* and more. Visit carriganak.wordpress.com or follow him on Twitter @carriganak for more info.

South African-born **GRANT SHIMMIN** lives in Christchurch, New Zealand, emerging from the destruction of major earthquakes 13 years ago, where derelict buildings still share space with the new popping up everywhere. He has work published or forthcoming in *Roi Faineant Press, Does it have Pockets?, The Hooghly Review, Dreich, Epistemic Lit, Querencia Press* and elsewhere. His social handles are: Twitter/X @shimmo23. Instagram: shimmonz

BART EDELMAN's poetry collections include *Crossing the Hackensack* (Prometheus Press), *Under Damaris' Dress* (Lightning Publications), *The Alphabet of Love* (Ren Hen Press), *The Gentle Man* (Ren Hen Press), *The Last Mojito* (Ren Hen Press), *The Geographer's Wife* (Ren Hen Press), *Whistling to Trick the Wind* (Meadowlark Press), and *This Body Is Never at Rest: New and Selected Poems 1993 – 2023* (Meadowlark Press). He has taught at Glendale College, where he edited *Eclipse,* a literary journal, and, most recently, in the MFA program at Antioch University, Los Angeles. His work has been widely anthologized in textbooks published by City Lights Books, Etruscan Press, Fountainhead Press, Harcourt Brace, Longman, McGraw-Hill, Prentice Hall, Simon & Schuster, Thomson/Heinle, the University of Iowa Press, Wadsworth, and others. He lives in Pasadena, California.

EVAN ELSASS is a writer from Columbus, Ohio. Presently, he resides in Long Beach, California, where he is pursuing a degree in English and Creative Writing at CSULB. His poetry has previously appeared in *Anacapa Review.* Evan is also the proud father of a large cat named Geo.

SAM CHRISTIE is a writer based in Wales, UK. He was longlisted for the Bridport Prize (Peggy Chapman-Andrews Award) 2021, was second place in the Writers' and Artists' Short Story Competition 2022, second in the Planet International Essay Competition 2022 and was third in the New Welsh Writers' Award 2023. He is currently writing a screenplay adapting his Bridport longlisted novel *Compass.*

MARIA BOURNE is a short story writer who shares her work on X and Instagram. She is currently working on her debut novel, a thrilling-yet-romantic tale of exploration and discovery on a magical planet with two suns. She lives in the sunny English countryside, where she is a devoted mother to her young daughter and she enjoys lots of woodland walks. She loves to curl up under a weighted blanket and write down the stories that come to her mind. X/Instagram: @ mariabourne_

JONATHAN WOO is a human being ('in case you were wondering' - from Jonathan). He has recently decided to pick up the pen after many years of only being a reader. He's interested in revealing stories that hide themselves in the ephemeral. His obsessions include Towers, photographs taken at dusk and the loch ness monster.

ANEETA SUNDARARAJ is an award-winning short story writer who created and developed a website called 'How to Tell a Great Story.' Her work has been featured in many publications. Her bestselling novel *The Age of Smiling Secrets* was shortlisted for the Book Award 2020 in Malaysia. In 2021, she successfully completed a doctoral thesis entitled 'Management of Prosperity Among Artistes in Malaysia.' She sometimes tweets at @httags

JON FAIN's recent publications include a pair of short stories in *A Thin Slice of Anxiety*, a flash fiction in *The Broadkill Review,* and micro fictions in *Blink-Ink, ScribesMICRO,* and *The Woolf.* He has stories in the 2023 anthologies *Tales of the Apocalypse* from Three Ravens Publishing and *Crimeucopia: Crank It Up!* from Murderous Ink Press. His chapbook of short fiction *Pass the Panpharmacon!* is available from Greying Ghost Press. He lives in Massachusetts. Twitter: @jonsfain

MARK KEANE has taught for many years in universities in North America and the UK. Recent short story fiction of his has appeared in *Avalon Literary Review, Bards and Sages Quarterly, Cape Magazine, Empyrean Literary Magazine, Seppuku, Shooter, untethered, Night Picnic, upstreet, Granfalloon, Liquid Imagination, Into the Void, Firewords,* and *Dog and Vile Short Fiction.* He lives in Edinburgh (Scotland).

LELAND HAMES (PAUL COOK) is the pen name of Paul Cook, a recently published short story author originally from the rural tip of Southern Illinois, now living on the outskirts of Chicago for the last 25 years. After his musical career was ended by a disabling "stroke of bad luck," he turned his creative focus to writing short fiction. He is a husband, father of two and is adept at one-handed typing. He has a weird and often dark sense of humor. Having become paralyzed on his left side, he is "all right" now he claims.

ASHLEY KAPLAN is a San Diego based photographer who specializes in working to empower the subjects she works with. She has been working as a photographer for eight years, and full time for two years. Ashley enjoys all things photography and the majority of the time you will find her with a camera in hand. If you catch her on the occasional moment without a camera in tow, you might find her running, hiking, painting, and hanging out with friends. To find more of Ashley's work, please find her on Instagram at @kaplan.photographyy

LOU GARZA is a 37-year-old artist, born in Fresno CA. Moved to San Diego in 1994. Essentially growing up in SD, he was surrounded with the beauty of the southern California city. Having found a love of art at a young age, doodling on the back of his test paper rather than taking the tests, this was surely a sign of the importance art would be in his life. Dropping out of college after taking all the interesting art classes available he set out to put his natural creative talent and skills he learned to the test. Taking time away from SD, he moved back to Fresno and worked for 3 years on building his artist portfolio. Creating music and playing in a band as well as earning a spot on the local Fresno State College emerging talent program on television. All the work he produced at this time was very personal to his young life and it culminated in his first solo art show at a local art gallery. Now being back in San Diego since 2015 he has been consistently producing art for himself and on commission, most recently he started his own mural painting business where he can produce the large works of art he always hoped he would. You can see more of his extensive artwork, as well as his video projects on Instagram @lougar or His mural work @mavssd

www.ingramcontent.com/pod-product-compliance
Lightning Source LLC
LaVergne TN
LVHW070138110826
845147LV00002B/281

9798999399182